For my son, Jack

First U.S. edition 2012

Library of Congress Cataloging-in-Publication Data is available.
Library of Congress Catalog Card Number 2011047003
ISBN 978-0-7636-5563-1

12 13 14 15 16 TTP 10 9 8 7 6 5 4 3 2

Printed in Huizhou, Guangdong, China

This book was typeset in Bauhaus Italic and Coronet MT.
The illustrations were created digitally.

Edited by Libby Hamilton and A.J. Wood
Designed by Mike Jolley

Templar Books

an imprint of Candlewick Press
99 Dover Street
Somerville, Massachusetts 02144
www.candlewick.com

JACK
AND THE BAKED
BEANSTALK

by
Colin
Stimpson

templar books
an imprint of Candlewick Press

Jack lived and worked in an old burger truck with his mom and his dog, Bella. Their sign read JACK'S FAST FOOD, which was funny because the truck had broken down a long time ago and it had stayed in the same place ever since, parked on the edge of the busy city.

Jack and his mom didn't really mind. They were proud of their little café. They kept the place clean, served tasty food, and always had plenty of happy customers.

One winter the city council decided to build an overpass so that more people could get to work even faster. The old road where Jack's café stood was to be closed.

At first things didn't seem very different. Jack and his mom were busy feeding the builders eggs and sausages, burgers and fries, and cups and cups of coffee. But when the overpass was finally complete, the workers went away.

All day long, traffic sped overhead as people hurried in and out of the city. No one stopped to visit the old burger truck anymore. The new road had swept the customers away. Soon Jack and his mom were down to their last few pennies.

"Go to the store and buy some milk and coffee beans, Jack," said Jack's mom, putting on a brave face. "Everybody likes a good cup of coffee."

On his way to the store, Jack met an old man who asked him why he looked so sad. Jack explained about the overpass and his burger truck.

"I think I can help you," said the old man thoughtfully. "Forget the coffee beans—these are magic baked beans. I wouldn't normally sell them, but you look like a boy who would know their true worth."

Now Jack had read enough fairy tales to know that you don't turn down an offer like that. Also, baked beans were his favorite food in the whole world, so he couldn't resist tasting some magic ones. Thanking the man, Jack exchanged his last pennies for the beans and ran home.

"You did what?" shouted his mom when Jack showed her the can.

"But Mom, they're magic baked beans. The old man promised," argued Jack, realizing how silly he sounded.

Furious, his mom threw the can out of the window and sent Jack straight to bed without any supper.

Early the next morning, Jack woke up to find his room bathed in a curious green light. Strange branches twisted in through the window. At the end of each shoot dangled a silver can of baked beans.

"It's a magic baked beanstalk," Jack whispered to Bella, trying not to wake his mother. "If I remember right, there should be heaps of treasure at the top!"

After quickly eating a breakfast of the best beans he had ever tasted, Jack crept outside.

"*Are* you ready, Bella?" said Jack, grabbing hold of a long green tendril. "Mom will be worried when she notices we're gone, but if this really is a magic beanstalk, she'll forget about being angry when we bring her back some treasure."

Up between the leaves they climbed, high into the sky. Finally Jack and Bella reached the top, just above the clouds. The last branch wound its way to the steps of the biggest castle Jack had ever seen.

Squeezing under the front door, Jack found himself in an enormous room. Suddenly there was a bone-shaking clunk, then another and another, followed by the sound of someone singing:

FEE-FI-FO-FUMMY,

I'M ALWAYS COUNTING MONEY.

BE IT SILVER OR BE IT GOLD,

IT'LL MAKE ME HAPPY—

OR SO I'M TOLD.

Sure enough, Jack could see towers of gold coins stacked up in front of a huge table and, behind it, an even more gigantic giant.

"Oh," whispered Jack. "I'd forgotten about that part of the story."

But just as Jack and Bella turned to run, the giant spotted them.

A huge hand reached down and scooped Jack and Bella high up in the air before dropping them on the table. In front of them was the most enormous chicken Jack had ever seen.

"We have visitors," boomed the giant.

"So I see," squawked the chicken.

"And we know just what to do with visitors, don't we?" said the giant. "Now you STAY THERE. I'll be back in a jiffy." And with that the giant grabbed a handful of the chicken's eggs and marched off to his kitchen. Soon the sound of clattering pots and pans was making the table tremble.

"Is he going to eat us, Chicken?" squeaked Jack.

"**Don't** be silly!" cackled the chicken. "He just wants to make you some lunch. He hasn't cooked for someone new in a long, long time."

As Jack watched, the giant switched on an enormous radio. Then, his foot tapping along to the sound of the music, he began to make the biggest omelet Jack had ever seen. While wonderful smells wafted into the room, the chicken told Jack about life in the castle.

"Every day, all day, the giant counts his money," she clucked. "He doesn't know what else to do with himself. It's hard for the radio—she's a magic one, you know. She can only play at lunchtime because the giant needs silence when he's counting."

Just then the giant appeared.

"Lunch is ready!" he cried cheerfully.

Over lunch Jack told the giant all about life at the bottom of the beanstalk, and the giant told Jack about his money. Jack thought having such treasure was fantastic, but the counting sounded a bit, well . . . boring.

"I do get pretty lonely up here," confessed the giant. "Would you consider staying? You could help me count and I could cook us tasty meals."

"Sorry," said Jack. "I just couldn't leave my mom. I should be getting back."

"Can I come with you?" sang a small voice. Jack and the giant turned to the radio in surprise. "I want to play songs all day long."

"And I've always wanted to stretch my wings," clucked the chicken.

The giant looked glum, but agreed that his friends deserved a change after all their years in the castle.

With a heavy heart, the giant walked them all to the top of the beanstalk.

"Are you sure you won't come with us?" asked Jack. "You could chase us!"

"I'd love to," said the giant sadly. "But, truth be told, I've always been a bit afraid of heights, and it looks like a long way down. I'd better stay here and count my gold."

So Jack and Bella climbed onto the chicken's back and, clutching the radio, began the long journey back to the ground.

"Good-bye! Good-bye!" hollered the giant, waving his handkerchief. "Do come again soon." But as he leaned out over the beanstalk, trying to catch a last glimpse of his friends, there was suddenly a loud CRACK. . . .

Snap! went the beanstalk, and down, down, down fell the giant— CRASH, BANG, WALLOP—right on top of the new overpass.

*C*ars skidded in all directions, but fortunately no one was hurt.

"Are you alright?" asked Jack, who had luckily reached the ground just in time.

"No," said the giant as a gigantic tear splashed onto the concrete below, then another and another. "Now that the beanstalk's broken, I can't go home. And without my money to count, I've got nothing to do. Whatever will become of me?"

"It isn't so bad," said Jack thoughtfully. "At least you're with your friends. Maybe if you try doing something you enjoy, you'll find it more fun than counting money."

And that is the story of how the Baked Beanstalk Café became the famous place it is today. It's much bigger than the old place, in almost every way.

If you're ever passing through, do stop in. Say hello to the giant chicken or listen to the jumbo radio that plays music all day. The baked beans and eggs are always free and, to top it all, they have a very, very famous cook.